D0407940

A TOLKIEN TREASURY

A TOLKIEN TREASURY

Edited by Alida Becker

Illustrations by Michael Green

Color illustrations by Tim Kirk

RUNNING PRESS
PHILADELPHIA • LONDON

A Running Press® Miniature Edition™

Printed in China

Library of Congress Cataloging-in-Publication Number 00-135504

ISBN 0-7624-0980-0

Special thanks to Marge Morrison.

This book may be ordered by mail from the publisher.
Please include $1.00 for postage and handling.
But try your bookstore first!

Running Press Book Publishers
125 South Twenty-second Street
Philadelphia, Pennsylvania 19103-4399

Visit us on the web!
www.runningpress.com

Enter into
a world of myth
and fantasy,
a place of Lords
and Ladies, hobbits
and nazguls.
Taste the food,
sing the songs, live
the legend!

"The world of knightly proving is a world of adventure."

Eric Auerbach,
Mimesis

"Middle Earth is a
world with a history and
a mythology all its own."

Alida Becker

"... certain people are dreamers and visionaries ... they embody values that the community cannot afford to forget."

Colin Wilson,
on Tolkien's belief

"Except feats of arms and love, nothing occurs in the courtly world."

Eric Auerbach,
Mimesis

Lament

by Ruth Berman

Treeherd counted the depths
of the wood.
Dryad, dryad, come back
to the oak.
Treeherd wandered by river
and hedge.
Nutmaid, nutmaid, turn in
the hazel.
Treeherd circled the snowline,
shivering.

Where are the greenhaired,
blossomcrowned,
Angular maidens with
barkbroken skin?
Treeherd wept like a
tapped maple
For hamadryads nowhere
to be seen
Twisted and beautiful,
in the green shadows.

Darkness wore
a cloak;
Wrapping for a
pale rider
Astride a black horse.

Nazgul

"O, Sauron made some Rings,
they were very useful things
And he only wanted One to keep
But Isildur took the One
just to have a little fun.
Sauron's finger was inside it,
what a creep!"

Translated by George Heap,
The Orcs' Marching Song

" . . . the values embodied
in *The Lord of the Rings* are
on the same level as those
in Yeats's fairy poems."

Colin Wilson

Smaug's Gems

by Maureen Bayha
and Alida Baker

Combine 1 cup of vanilla wafer crumbs, 1 cup of confectioners' sugar, 1 cup of chopped nuts, and 1 tablespoon of cocoa. Add 2 tablespoons of light corn syrup and ¼ cup of whisky. Mix well and shape into 1-inch balls. Roll in confectioners' sugar and place in an air-tight container. Store in the refrigerator.

Moon-silver
beauty;

Soft song bringing
ancient tears

To the
elven-lords.

Luthien Tinuviel

Lord Rohan

The Mountain King returned,
the river flowed with gold,
And Mr. Baggins turned at last
back toward his hobbit hole.
Returning from adventure, from
war and dragon's lair,
He found Lobelia walking off
with all his silverware.

from *Smaug the Magic Dragon*

"*The Lord of the Rings* is
a criticism of the modern
world and of the values of
technological civilization."

Colin Wilson

The gnarled and
twisted trees so huge,

the man so small
he seems a halfling;

he stands amid roots
which rise to his knees.

J.R. Christopher,
A Baroque Memorial:
J.R.R. Tolkien

"Tolkien's work involved both writing definitions and deciding on the origins of the words that had been chosen. In many cases, the sources of a particular word were based as much on guessing as on scholarship."

Joan McClusky

". . . his wholly original
story of adventure among
goblins, elves, and dragons . . .
gives . . . the impression of
a well-informed glimpse
into the life of a wide other
world . . . "

The New Statesman and Nation

"O'er all the lands their
fair folk trod,
The final eventide has come,
And those who wandered,
silver-shod,
Have faded from the changing land.
The march of man has pushed
them from
Their forest lands and verdant sod
Until at last they must succumb
To forces they cannot withstand."

Ted Johnstone

"The Americans took
Middle-earth for their own.
They learned to read, write,
and speak the languages;
they drew maps and posters;
they formed clubs and printed
bulletins, newsletters, and
magazines. An amazed and
uncomprehending world gaped."

Philip W. Helms

Firework's End

by Ruth Berman

"'I hope you'll say a word about his
fireworks,' said Sam."
Brief explosions of gold and green,
Coral branching into a moment's reef,
And a blue fan which, opening,
Is gone.
As each flares against the dark
It lights up the clouds of floating ash,
Immense, faint streaks of patchy light
Across the surface of deep heaven.
The moon drifts up, and as it

clears the trees,
The wizard leans upon his staff
To put his squibs away.
Something he knows the moon
knows, too.
The night grows cold.
Points of water gather into drops
And damp a wizard's cloak and hat.
Even wizards grow weary
and long for bed.
The stars in the depth of the sky
are bright
When the moon is down.

Beorn's Honey Nut Cake

by Maureen Bayha
and Alida Becker

Put 1½ cups of cottage cheese through a strainer. Mix the strained cottage cheese with 1½ tablespoons of sifted flour, ¼ teaspoon of salt, 3 table-spoons of sour cream, 3 beaten egg yolks, ¾ cup of honey, 1 tablespoon of butter, 1 tablespoon of lemon juice, the rind of 1 lemon, and ½ cup of wheat germ. Fold in 3 egg whites, stiffly beaten. Butter a 9-inch-square cake pan. Sprinkle the bottom of the pan with ⅛ cup of wheat germ. Pour the batter into the pan and top with ⅛ cup of wheat germ and ½ cup of chopped nuts. Bake in a preheated 375-degree oven for 30 minutes.

"Tolkien was a
precocious child—
he had invented
three or four languages
by the age of ten."

Joan McClusky

Tall, straight,
leather-hard;

Blood of past
and future kings,

With a
broken sword.

Aragorn

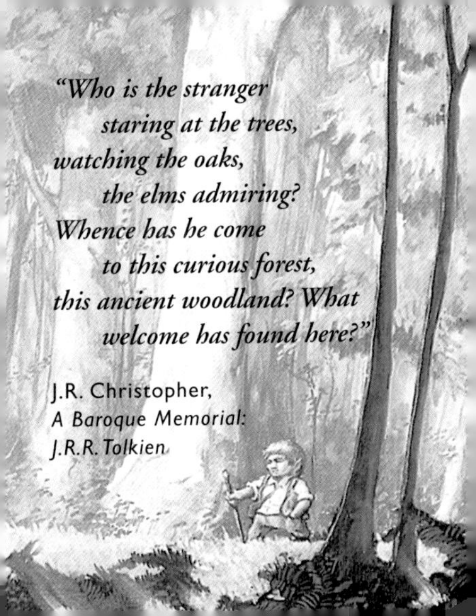

"Who is the stranger
staring at the trees,
watching the oaks,
the elms admiring?
Whence has he come
to this curious forest,
this ancient woodland? What
welcome has found here?"

J.R. Christopher,
A Baroque Memorial:
J.R.R. Tolkien

"The hobbits are just rustic English people, made small in size because it reflects the generally small reach of their imagination."

J.R.R. Tolkien

Snowy brows,
blue eyes;
A flash of fire
and thunder—
The old grey pilgrim.

Gandalf

Gandalf

Shire Pudding

by Maureen Bayha
and Alida Becker

Mix together 1 cup of milk, 2 eggs, 1 cup of flour, and 1 teaspoon of salt in a blender. Put 3 tablespoons of hot beef or lamb drippings in a 9-inch glass pie plate. Pour the batter into the middle of the drippings. Bake in a preheated 425-degree oven for 15 minutes. Reduce the heat to 350 degrees and continue baking until the pudding is puffy and brown.

Elven Brooch

"The HAZEL with filberts is
formed into thickets,
and wisdom is his who wins
to the center
to feed on the filberts, to fill
his deep longing,
to know the nine Hazels
nigh Connla's Well
which flower as they're nutting,
all fairness, all knowledge."

J.R. Christopher,
A Baroque Memorial:
J.R.R. Tolkien

"No more the fair Galadriel
Will sing in green Lothlorien;
The empty halls of Rivendell,
Deserted, silent, thick with dust,
Recall the empty hours when
They stood as lonely citadel
Against the coming age of Men,
But fell, as Elrond knew they must."

Ted Johnstone,
The Passing of the Elven-kind

"What so impressed me on that first reading was the self-containedness of Tolkien's world."

Colin Wilson

"Tolkien's humor and scholarship combine to make him a popular lecturer."

Joan McClusky

"Black against the pall of
cloud, there rose up a huge
shape of shadow, impenetrable,
lightning-crowned, filling
all the sky."

The Lord of the Rings

Beneath the
black crown;

Red, in a skull
of blue fire,

The eye burns
with hate.

Sauron

" . . . Mr. Tolkien has
succeeded more completely
than any previous writer
in this genre in using the
traditional properties of
the Quest, the heroic journey,
the Numinous Object,
the conflict between Good
and Evil . . . "

W.H. Auden

We called it his last work,
but *The Silmarillion*
was his first work as well;
it must have filled and
coloured every part of
his life for 60 years."

William Cater

"The reader walks through any Middle-earth landscape with a security of recognition that woos him on to believe anything that happens. Familiar but not too familiar, strange but not too strange. This is the master rubric that Tolkien bears always in mind when creating the world of the epic."

Paul Kocher

"I cordially dislike allegory in all its manifestations, and always have done so since I grew old and wary enough to detect its presence."

J.R.R. Tolkien

Warg

"Evil, that is, has
every advantage but
one—it is inferior
in imagination."

W.H. Auden

"Tolkien spoke of the need
to escape the troubles of our
modern world into another
world where even wizards
and dragons were much more
appealing, and where good
and evil were more simply
and clearly defined."

Joan McClusky

TIM KIRK

"The shadows of the fading age

Grew long across the fields of gold;

The Elven-lords, each silent, sage,

Had left the flow-ring mallorn trees.

For them the world was growing old—

Though mankind saw a turning page—

The fair folk left their last freehold

And passed beyond the Sundering Seas."

Ted Johnstone,
The Passing of the Elven-kind

"To present the conflict between Good and Evil as a war in which the good side is ultimately victorious is a ticklish business."

W.H. Auden

"In Middle-earth
there is a tavern on the
Eastern Road.

There travelers will find
its tables full of cheer;

And when the inn-
keeper brings the beer,

He may bend an ear."

The song *Middle-earth*

"... Tolkien certainly
enjoys creating a scene,
revelling in it. This is
certainly the basic
strength and charm
of the book."

Colin Wilson on
The Lord of the Rings

"And Cirdan wrought them ships
which bore
Them from Havens o'er the sea
And watched them sail for fairer
shore
And leave the world of mortal man
In which no place for them could be.
And in this world they stay no more,
But dwell in Elvenhome the Free
As fair as when the world began."

Ted Johnstone,
The Passing of the Elven-kind

T. KIRK

". . . our flesh and bones
and souls are cold here."

Marci Helms Knisley

"(Middle-earth) is simply
an old fashioned word for
the world we live in, as
imagined and surrounded by
the ocean . . . at a different
stage of imagination."

J.R.R. Tolkien

"Tolkien began *The Lord of the Rings* in 1937; he worked on it for eleven years before he had completed the first draft."

Joan McClusky

"Over the past twenty-five years, J.R.R. Tolkien has become a respected figure in the literary world."

Alida Becker

“Good can
imagine the possibility
of being evil . . . ”

W.H. Auden

"The hobbits are a not quite human race who inhabit an imaginary country called the Shire . . . "

Edmund Wilson

"There are streaks of imagination: the ancient tree-spirits, the Ents, with their deep eyes, twiggy beards, rumbly voices; the Elves, whose nobility and beauty is elusive and not quite human."

Edmund Wilson

Ent

"A newcomer to Middle-earth quickly finds himself engulfed in a vast and sometimes confusing world with a past as lengthy and diverse as our own."

Douglas Kendall

". . . real taste for fairy stories was awakened by philology on the threshold of manhood, and quickened to full life by war."

J.R.R. Tolkien

"The children
who swallow the star
are the poets—like
Yeats or Tolkien—
who become
wanderers between
two worlds."

Colin Wilson

"When evil ceases to
be concentrated but
becomes spread thin
through the world,
we are no longer in
the black and white
of mythology . . . "

William Cater

"There can be no doubt that Tolkien himself is emotionally committed to this fairy tale picture of peaceful rural life; it is not intended solely for the children."

Colin Wilson

"J.R.R. Tolkien
was a literary giant, an
epos unto himself."

Kenneth John Atchity

"As his life went on, the
mythology and poetry
in my father's work
sank down behind
the philosophy and
theology in it . . ."

Christopher Tolkien

"The excitement of the book lies in the journey, and in Tolkien's invention."

Colin Wilson

"Comparison to the Bible, on literary grounds, is not exaggerated since the aesthetic that guides both is the same stark combination of mythology and morality that lends the credibility of truth."

Kenneth John Atchity

". . . his people lamented him ever after and took no king again."

The Silmarillion

This book has been bound
using handcraft methods, and
Smyth-sewn to ensure durability.

The dust jacket and
interior were designed by
Frances J. Soo Ping Chow.

The text was edited by
Danielle McCole.

The text was set in
Adobe Garamond and Gill Sans.